The Convict Children

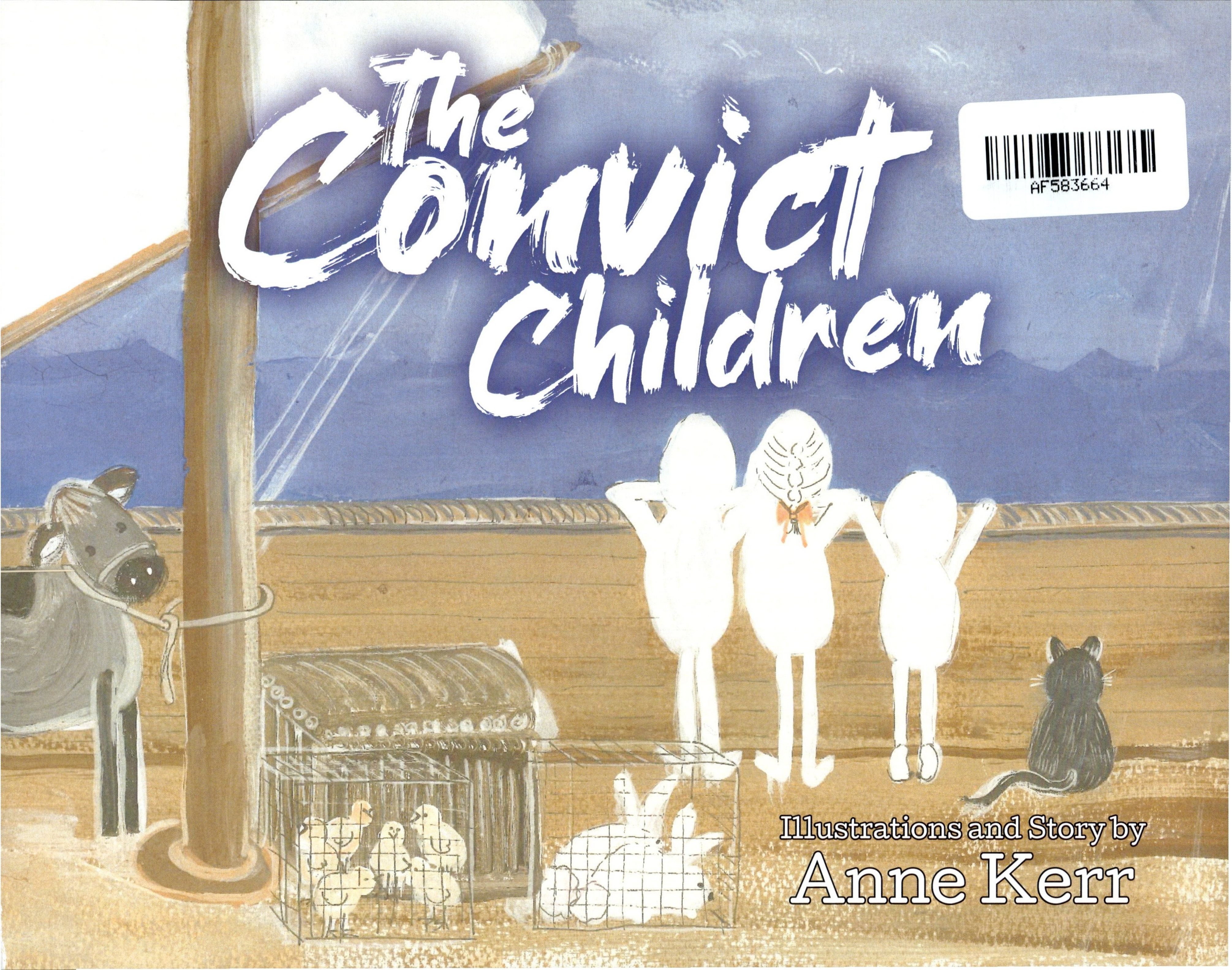

Illustrations and Story by

Anne Kerr

We acknowledge the Traditional Owners of the land on which we publish books,
the Quandamooka people, and pay our respects to Elders past, present and emerging.

Published by

38/1631 Wynnum Road
Tingalpa Qld 4173
Australia
www.boolarongpress.com.au

First published 2024

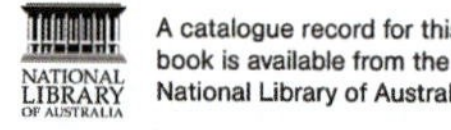

ISBN: 9780975650813 (paperback)

Printed and bound by Watson Ferguson & Company, Tingalpa, Australia

This is a story about Australia. It is a true story.

Lightning flashed and thunder cracked and boomed.
The ship rose and fell with the huge waves that tossed it about.

The children covered their ears. Surely, tonight the ship they were on would sink! They clung to each other in fear. All they wanted to do was to go back home to their families. Back home to England.

They were scared. They huddled together beneath the decks of the sailing ship. Above them they could hear the thumping and banging of the sailors' feet as they ran from one end of the ship to the other, shouting orders.

These were the convict children. Put together in a cage, like animals, at the very bottom of the ship. Beside them was a bigger cage crammed full of convict men. Everyone groaned as the ship reared up and then smashed down into the hollow of the waves. They all wanted to go home.

Finally, the storm ended and the ship settled down. Those convicts who could fell asleep. Others just stared hopelessly and wondered how long they would be on this journey. The children began to cry. There was no mother or father to hug them or tell them that they would be alright. They were cold and wet. They had no shoes. Only the lucky ones had a coat to keep them warm. They were dirty, smelly and very hungry. It was horrible.

The children thought of their homes in England. They had been hungry there too. So hungry, they had snatched bread or fruit from the markets to eat. So cold, they had stolen shoes and coats to keep themselves warm. They had been caught by the police and put on this ship for doing the wrong thing.

There were 10 other ships with theirs. This was the First Fleet, and whether the children liked it or not, they were being sent far away over the seas to a strange great southland called Terra Australis.

Ships of The First Fleet
Golden Grove
Lady Penrhyn
Friendship
HMS Supply
HMS Sirius
Borrowdale
Fishburn
Charlotte
Alexander
Scarborough
Prince of Wales

The children heard the sailors talking about the strange animals that lived in this new land. They said there were giant mouse-like creatures that grew a pocket to put their babies in! These mice hopped on strong back legs. There were giant birds with long necks like a giraffe. They could run but not fly.

There were bright blue skies that stretched up and out, and a hot, hot sun that blazed down and sizzled the ground. The sailors said that this new land was empty. No one else lived there. The children could not imagine this. Where they came from, there were people everywhere.

The First Fleet took eight months to reach the eastern side of Australia. The days on the ship stretched on and on. The animals on board grew restless. Sometimes, the convict children were allowed up on deck to breathe the fresh air. They saw the big sea stretched out far before them, meeting the sky. Above them, the ship's sails flapped in the breeze. Behind them, the other ships of the fleet followed, rising up and down in the ocean swell.

This new land was far away from England. The children wondered if this journey would ever end. Sadly, they began to understand that they would never be going back to their families. Suddenly, a sailor, way up in the crow's nest, shouted out, "Land Ahoy!"

The convict children watched from the deck. So this was Australia, their new homeland! They had finally arrived. In the distance were bush and mountains that stretched as far as they could see.

The ship's anchors dropped with a splash into the sea. Rowboats dropped from the ship's side, loaded with cargo to be taken to shore. There were crates of nails, axes, fishing nets, tents, pots and saucepans. There were sacks of food and seeds that would be needed to grow food in this new country. Even the cows and horses were lifted out and lowered into the boats to be rowed to the beach.

List of some of the Livestock, Provisions, Plants and Seeds that were on the ships of the First Fleet

10 forges • 700 steel spades • 700 iron shovels • 700 garden hoes • 700 West Indian hoes • 700 grubbing hoes • 700 felling axes • 700 hatches • 747,000 nails • 700 hinges & hooks • 6 carts • 40 corn mills • 40 wheelbarrows • 12 ploughs • 12 smith's bellows • 30 grindstones • 330 iron pots • 4 timber carriages • 14 fishing nets • 14 chains for timber carriages • 5,448 squares of crown grass • 200 canvas beds • 62 cauldrons of coal • 80 carpenter's axes • 20 shipwright's axes • 600lbs coarse sugar • 1001lbs Indian Sago • 1 sml cask of raisons • 61lbs spices • 3 snuffers • 48 spinning brasses • 7doz razors • Bible, Prayer book etc • 6 bullet moulds • 700 steel spades • 175 claw hammers • 140 augurs • 700 gimlets • 504 saw files • 300 chisels • 6 butcher's knives • 100 prs scissors • 30 box rulers • 100 plain measures • 50 pickaxes • 50 helves for DO • 700 wooden bowls • 700 DO platters • 5 sets of smith's tools • 20 pit saws • 700 clasp knives • 500 tin plates • 60 padlocks • 50 hay forks • 42 splitting wedges • 8,000 fish hooks • 48doz fishing lines • 12 brick moulds • 36 mason's chisels • 6 horse harnesses • 12 ox-bowls • 8doz lbs sewing twine • 3 sets of ox furniture • 20 bushels of seed barley • 1 piano • 10 bushells of Indian seed corn • transport jack • 12 baskets of garden seed • coarse

thread (blue/white) • ventilators for water & wine • hoses • windsails • 24 spinning whorls • 1 set candlestick makers • carbines • bulkhead beds • 9 hackies for flax • 9 hackies pins • 3 flax dresser brushes • 127doz combs • 18 coils of whale line • 6 harpoons • 12 lances • shoe leather • 305 prs of women's shoes • 40 tents for women convicts • 6 bundles of ridge poles • 11 bundles of stand poles • 2 chests of pins & mallets • 4 cows • 1 bull 1 portable canvas house (Gov • Phillip) • 18 turkeys • 29 geese • 35 ducks • 122 fowls • 87 chickens • kittens • puppies • 4 mares • 2 stallions • 1 bull calf • 44 sheep • 19 goats • 32 hogs • 5 rabbits • Gov. Phillip's greyhound dogs • Rev. John's cats • mill spindles with 4 crosses • 121 women's caps • 2 cases of mill bills & picks • 1 case of mill brashes • hammocks • pears • fig trees • apples • 606 women's jackets • 589 women's petticoats • 327prs of women's stockings • 250 handkerchiefs • marine's clothes • bamboos • sugar cane • quinces • strawberries • oak & myrtle trees • 135 tierces of beef • 165 tierces of pork • 50 puncheons of bread • 116 casks of pease • 110 firkins of butter • 8 bram of rice • 10 prs of handcuffs and tools • 1 chest of books • 5 puncheons of rum • 300 gallons of brandy • 23 tons of drinking water • 5 casks of oatmeal • 12 bags of rice • 140 women's hats • 1 machine for dress flax • 220 doz lbs of cotton candles • 168 doz lbs of mould candles • 44 tons of tallow • 5440 drawers • 2 millstone's spindles • 800 sets of bedding • 1 loom for weaving canvas • 800 sets of bedding • 2780 woollen jackets • 40 camp kettles • 26 marguees for married officers • 200 wood canteens • 448 barrels of flour • 60 bushels of seed wheat • 381 women's shifts • Plants & seeds: banana • cocoa • coffee • cotton • eugenia • guava • ipecacuanha • lemon • orange • prickly pear • Spanish reed • tamarind

Source: First Fleet Fellowship, Victoria Inc.

The children began to feel excited. But WAIT!
Over there in the trees. Who was that in the shadows watching?

PEOPLE! There were people ... already here.

This is a copy of my great, great maternal grandfather Jesse's Ticket of Leave. He was 14 years old when convicted of burglary in England. He was given a life sentence to be served in Australia. Two years after conviction, he was on the transport ship Norfolk with 180 other convicts, landing in Botany Bay. He was 16 years old by then and worked in a government job for Mr W. Sturgeon until he was granted a Ticket of Leave 11 years after conviction.

This entitled him to land in the Bathurst area of New South Wales. He was not allowed to move freely to other parts of Australia, nor to return back to his homeland of England. Jesse married while he was a convict. He and Sarah had nine children.

TICKET OF LEAVE.

No. 34/1539 31 Decr 1834.

Prisoner's No. ....

Name .... Jesse Dibley

Ship .... Norfolk (1)

Master .... Greig

Year 1825

Native Place ...... Woodhurst

Trade or Calling ... Ploughman

Offence ....

Place of Trial ..... Sussex Assizes

Date of Trial....... 26 July 1823

Sentence.......... Life

Year of Birth...... 1809

Height.......... 5 feet 5 1/4 Inches

Complexion .... Freckled

Hair .... Red

Eyes .... Grey

General Remarks...

Allowed to remain in the District of Bathurst

On recommendation of Sydney Bench,

Dated 31 October 1834

SEE OVER

About the Author

Anne Kerr has been a kindergarten teacher for 34 years. This book follows on from three previous books—*Sorry, Sorry*, *Walking to Corroboree* (a co-authored venture with Adnyamathanha woman and friend, Rhanee) and *The Didgeridu Crew*. While *The Convict Children* is from the perspective of the convict children and their forced separation from family and all that was familiar to them, it highlights their resilience in the face of harsh, cruel conditions and treatment by the adults in their lives. The presumption by the British Government that Australia was empty of people and therefore free to "take over" also comes under the microscope, leading, hopefully, to further research and discussion to determine the truth It's an uncomfortable history we have here in Australia. This is a shared history that can foster a shared sense of belonging if we are brave enough to explore it and pass it on to new generations.

Other resources: To download First Fleet facts and worksheets go to: **Kidsconnect.com**

Captain James Cook wrote in his journal: "they (the Australian Aboriginal) may appear to be the most wretched people upon the earth: but in reality they are far more happier than (we) Europeans ... They live in Tranquility which is not disturbed by the Inequality of Condition: the Earth and Sea of their own accord furnishes them with all things necessary for life."

"All they seemed to want," said Cook, "was for us to be gone."

Excerpt from *Aliens and Savages* by Janeen Webb and Andrew Enstice. Harper Collins Pub. 1998